A Dog Called Corporal

JACK CHAMPION

Copyright © 2022 Jack Champion

All rights reserved.

Although this is inspired by true events, this is a work of fiction and names, places and incidents have often been used in a fictitious manner.

Any resemblance to real people, living or dead, or actual events is therefore entirely coincidental.

All rights reserved. This book or any portion thereof may not be reproduced or used in any manner whatsoever without the express written permission of the publisher except for the use of brief quotations in a book review.

ISBN: 9798435776270

Email: masterdonpublishing@gmail.com

DEDICATION

To my three sons.
May you never have to fight in any wars.

And to the animal companions no longer with me.
The dog, and the cat who thought it was a dog.
Still loved and never forgotten.

CONTENTS

1	Two Shillings and Sixpence	11
2	Promotion	27
3	Miners	40
4	The Tunnel	51
5	Duty	62
6	Glory	77
	Epilogue	92

Author's Note

This story (in its most basic form) has been handed down my family for several generations.

My Great Aunt (her name has been changed in this story along with a few details) served as a war nurse in WW1, and she never forgot the real Bill and Corporal.

A remarkable woman, Great Aunt Annie told many tales of her life at the Western Front, winning a Red Cross medal for her heroism, but this story of a man and his dog remains probably one of the most poignant of all of her wartime accounts. She always had a tear in her eye when she told it.

I plan to write some more of Annie's adventures one day. In the meantime, I bring you the story of Bill and Corporal.

I have fictionalised a few details and incidents (as well as characters) for the sake of the story, but the essential story remains true.

Based on a true story.

1.
TWO SHILLINGS AND SIXPENCE

TWO SHILLINGS AND SIXPENCE. That was the bounty the recruiting officer received when he signed up William 'Bill' Higgins to fight with the British Army in France. No matter that William was just a spindly lad and barely looked his age of 17, let alone 18, the minimum age that he should have been.

William, known as "Bill" by his friends, had first discovered a thirst for adventure and glory when army recruiters had passed through the sleepy little hillside village of Sunnington Down in Berkshire during the long hot summer of 1915. And no one was going to stop him from enlisting to fight for his country. Not his father, Joseph, who was a respected village elder and the gamekeeper on Lord Sunnington's Ascot Heath Estate, nor his mother Margaret, a maid at Ascot Heath Manor. Bill was going to have a go at Fritz, whatever anyone said. He was going to do England proud. He would make darn well sure of it.

Dressed in their Sunday church clothes, Bill and his best friend John Padfield had eagerly marched off with the recruiting sergeant to the army depot at Windsor.

Not even so much as a fond farewell was said to their parents or siblings. They'd be sent a note from the barracks.

The two boys were caught up in the thrill of it all, and for the want of easy money, the recruiting sergeant had turned a blind eye to the two boys so obviously being underage. But then, it wasn't all about money from the recruitment bounty: the army desperately needed soldiers.

England and France had been at war with Germany for over a year, and the fighting on the Western Front had been fierce. Newspaper reports were full of the battles, the valiant attempts by British and Indian Army soldiers to force back the spike-helmeted Hun. The casualty lists posted on town hall notice boards up and down the country made for grim reading. But despite this, what young man could resist the call of Lord Kitchener's "Your Country Needs You" poster and what patriot could not be moved by cries of God save the King? After all, General Kitchener was the hero of the British Empire's colonial wars in Sudan and South Africa, the things of daring adventure novels. So, Bill and John had marched boldly off to war with daydreams of daring-do and heroism filling their young minds. That was seven months ago now, and everything had changed since then.

Bill now sat shivering at the bottom of a mud-filled, rat-infested trench, alongside his friend John and the other men of the Berkshire Pals Battalion. All were from towns and villages from across the Thames Valley county. Some were brothers, others were cousins and friends, all joining on the promise that they could fight with their 'pals' and not be scattered throughout the army.

Bill huddled up bored, his head resting on a sandbag. Today was a waiting day just like the other waiting days, a cold, grey and monotonous morning. A low wet mist covered them, muffling the sound of distant guns. It wasn't just the cold; it was the wet. Infernal wet. The long hot summer of 7 months before now seemed another lifetime away. It was another lifetime away.

Bill closed his eyes momentarily, trying to remember how the sun felt on his freckles as he and John Padfield lazily lay by the sparkling village duck pond, the ducks honking all about them. His eyes squeezed together more tightly as he imagined what Sunnington Down looked like bathed in sunlight, how the neat redbrick workers' cottages gleamed, and the Norman village church shone, and what the apple blossom looked like in the orchards. There was no better place in summer. It was a beautiful corner of England: *his* England.

In his mind, Bill inhaled the place's scent along with the heady scent of wisteria around his mother's door. The ginger tomcat was napping again on the window ledge, its purr so loud it was no wonder it didn't wake itself. Mother's door was open, and inside he could smell familiar baking smells—

Somebody now brushed past him, causing his eyes to spring open momentarily and his vision of England to vanish as quickly as a shifting shadow. It was a tease every time he returned there, but it was all he had to hold onto.

He was planning to close his eyes to return to the long hot summer, but before he did, his eyes now settled lazily on his best friend. John had aged considerably, his face now reflecting an old man's. He looked more like his dad now, Bill mused. Forty. It was the worry in the posture. The weight on his shoulders. He guessed he probably looked the same.

John huddled nearby, using the short stub of an army-issue pencil to scrawl out a postcard to his mother. Hardly a 'Wish You Were Here', but it may as well have been as it was full of equally banal chatter. *"I'm all right. I hope Sissy is okay. Love to Pip."*

On the front of the postcard was a picture of a soldier praying beside joint flags of Britain and France. Praying that this God-forsaken war would soon be over just like they all were. Chance would be a fine thing.

The light in John's blue eyes had dulled, so now his eyes looked as grey as the rest of them in the trench, even his skin seeming to have that pallor. Bill guessed he looked the same as his mate. They all did here. Ghosts of the boys they had once been. Here for glory.

They hadn't seen any fighting yet. Just mud.

Bill noticed the shoulders of all the men in C Company straightening up, even while they remained sloping in position, and knew without looking that the Captain and his second in command were now in sight, which meant the sarge was not far behind.

Captain Sidney Wellsworth-Pike commanded C Company of the Berkshire Pals, and his second in command was a fellow toff called Lieutenant Anthony Smythe. Both had suspended their studies in Classics at Oxford University and signed up for the duration. They had played Officer Corps at Eton and were now playing war here in this trench. In their minds at least, They were alright as higher-ups went, not that Bill had much experience of the higher-ups, only heard what the other men in other companies had to say about theirs. Toffs, as a rule, did not garner much respect. Obedience, yes, undoubtedly, for blind obedience came with the sign-up call. The sergeants on the other hand were another breed. They were not just to be respected but to be feared. They were real soldiers.

Captain Wellsworth-Pike was prematurely bald, in that posh kind of way that perhaps came with inbreeding. It was hard to believe the man was only 22. He had an earnest expression that always hinted he'd rather be reading Homer than a map. He also always seemed to squint. It was hard to believe he did not need glasses. Perhaps he did when no one was looking, Bill mused.

Lieutenant Smythe was just 19 years old. His youth was a sign of the high casualty rate among officers and men. He seemed even greener than Bill, if that was possible. Although muscular, it was clear from his all-around demeanour that he'd never done a day's manual labour in his life, and he seemed made for the polo field than the trenches as he moved with a grace befitting an equestrian. But then who was made for trenches apart from rats? Sergeants, perhaps. They seemed made for this place.

Red-faced Platoon Sergeant Albert Keane was a career soldier, a man to be respected, one to be even feared. Sergeant Keane had seen battle on the frontiers of India and even in China during the Boxer Rebellion of 1900. And he had the campaign medals and ribbons to prove it. Keane was widely respected by both men and officers alike and was directly in charge of Bill's platoon. He now followed behind the Captain and Lieutenant as he, just like his men, knew his place.

Squinting again, Captain Wellsworth-Pike looked in Bill's direction, and Bill found himself straightening up a little in spite of himself. There was the barest of looks of recognition from the Captain, then a nod to Bill as if to say "at ease". Then the Captain turned on his heel and headed into a bunker with the lieutenant.

"Pick yourself up, lad." A larger-than-life Sergeant Keane now loomed over Bill. He looked down at the pimply-faced youth, steel combat helmet jammed on his head, leather straps dangling either side of his sunken cheeks. At least the boy's Pattern Service Dress tunic and trousers were not filthy. The thick woollen tunic was khaki in colour and had a number of pockets for personal items, paybook and an internal pocket sewn into the right flap of the lower tunic for a field dressing. His calves and ankles were covered by the traditional puttees. These were a long and thin piece of cloth wrapped tightly in a spiral to provide support and some protection.

The Sergeant took a particularly hard look at Bill's general service hobnailed ammunition boots. Not exactly clean, but they would do. The boy was passable.

The Sergeant shook his head in some despair, but then they were in the trenches, not behind the lines resting. Plus, he realised with a sigh, that all the men of the battalion were so young, not career soldiers. The oldest man in the platoon was just 22, and that was the Captain, while the youngest of the men were Higgins here and then John Padfield. They had just celebrated their eighteenth birthdays a few weeks before, still a year shy of the official age for serving in the British Army. However, whatever their age, they were all now soldiers in His Majesty's army, and that was good enough for Sergeant Keane.

"I have a new assignment for you, Private Higgins. Grab your rifle, buckle on your webbing and follow me. Quickly now!"

Bill, doing his best to disguise his chattering jaw, leapt up to obey. He shot a look at John, who nodded, his face impassive. They both knew what an assignment could mean. John's eyes, without words, said: best of British, mate.

Bill and the Sarge traced their way through the trench system, squeezing past men cleaning their rifles, some carrying ammunition boxes and one or two stumbling with cooking pots called dixies full of food. A cold meal was routine for the men in the trenches. No matter how the cooks tried to get hot food to the front, it never happened. The field kitchens were just too far away from the front lines.

Sergeant Keane motioned Bill to follow him into a smaller communication trench that led to the rear area. After about an hour, they emerged into a small clearing bustling with soldiers, many tucking into their breakfast, sipping sweet tea, and generally making ready for the day ahead. NCOs shouted here and there.

Why NCOs always shouted at the top of their voices was a mystery to Bill. Perhaps it was just an army tradition as sometimes there simply seemed no need. He would have asked Sergeant Keane but knew such a question would not be welcomed, and Keane was a stern man. "Do what I tell you, nothing more, nothing less, is what you'll do". This was the welcome to basic training speech they had all received from the Company sergeant. Short and sharp. To the point.

"Where are we going, Sarge?" Bill ventured as he scrambled to keep up with Keane but received only a noncommittal grunt in reply.

Just then, a small motor ambulance vehicle pulled up next to them, and the lean, dark-haired driver leaned out.

"You Keane?" he asked in an accent unknown to Bill.

The man was in a British Army uniform: thick woollen tunic and trousers, dyed khaki, a light shade of tan with a slight yellowish tinge. On the right sleeve of his tunic was a prominent red cross armband. The same symbol was painted on the side of the motor ambulance. But this man wasn't British.

Bill frowned, wondering if he was from the colonies. That would explain the accent.

Dismissing the thought, Bill stared at the vehicle the man was driving. He was more used to horse-drawn wagons. Of course, he had heard of motor vehicles even in his small village of Sunnington Down, Lord Sunnington even had one - a fine Rolls Royce, no less - and was known to whizz down the country lanes in his making Bill more than once wobble on his bicycle as he sped past, but this was the first time that Bill had ever been so up close and personal to one. It certainly was impressive, he thought. The noise the engine made was loud, and clouds of noxious black smoke billowed from underneath it. It made him cough as the oily fumes caught in his throat.

If it was impressive to a country boy like Bill, to Sergeant Keane, it was a real marvel of technology in the service of the army. A godsend. Just like the Vickers machine guns, which could provide the same firepower as more than a hundred soldiers in as many seconds. Just after the outbreak of the war in 1914, Keane had been wounded and carried from the battlefield to a rear aid station on the back of a donkey. Every single sway and jolt had sent him deeper into the abyss. Horror stories abounded of wounded soldiers transported for hours to the nearest railway station, laid out on straw in a cattle car open to the elements, and then sent towards the nearest city with a hospital. With no water, no bandages, and no food, some in agony, others unconscious, many died on the journey. Keane had been lucky. He still had the scars to prove it. But by God, that ambulance would have lessened his nightmare of a donkey ride.

Sergeant Keane shot a glance across to Private Higgins and could see the fascination shining in the young boy's eyes.

"Come on, you limeys never seen a motor vehicle before or what?" The man with the strange accent called out mockingly.

"Sod off, Yank!" Keane retorted in a humorous tone.

Bill looked at the sergeant and saw him smiling. Keane smiling! Wait until John and the lads heard about this. Then he turned to the ambulance driver: a Yank. So he was an American. That explained the accent then.

"In you get, Private Higgins. This is where I leave you. You'll get your new orders at the field hospital."

Keane slapped Bill's shoulder. Then slapped it again as if for luck. His voice became deeper. "Good luck, lad."

Field hospital? New orders? Bill was baffled at this unexpected turn of events. But in the army, you didn't think, you followed orders without question, and so he climbed into the bucket-like wooden bench seat next to the Yank.

Keane turned away and headed back to the opening of the communication trench. He turned and raised a large calloused hand adieu and then disappeared from sight.

Once inside, Bill could feel the vibrations from the motor. He wondered if the spindly wheels could carry the whole structure of the ambulance or if it would shake itself to pieces in the ruts and holes which potted the dirt roads.

Bill steadied his rifle between his legs and glanced down.

Much to his surprise, curled up there between him and the driver was a dog. It had a perfectly fitted white canvas cloth wrapped around it, a bit like the horse rugs used at the manor's stables during winter. On the white cloth was a red cross.

The dog blinked up at him, its chocolate-brown eyes warm and trusting. For the briefest of moments, Bill felt human again. A man and not a number lost somewhere in the misery that was Northern France.

Bill peered at the dog, lost for words a moment. The dog blinked at him again, as if he knew him inside and out and had already met him and needed absolutely no introduction. Its eyes spoke of an uncanny intelligence.

"An Airedale Terrier?" murmured Bill. 'What's his name?"

The dog was an Airedale Terrier, just like the one his best friend John had back home in Sunnington Down. Dense, curly coat, black and tan in colour, Airedales were intelligent animals. For a moment, Bill felt a deep pang of homesickness that ran all the way through to his core.

Back home, the warm redbrick buildings would be bathed in the winter sun, and John's dog, Pip, would be snoozing in front of the fire, wondering where his master was and wondering when he would come home. Smoke would be puffing out from the chimney, and John's mother and sister, Sissy, would likely be baking in the kitchen. Something delicious, Bill thought, something like roast beef and Yorkshire pudding-– Bill's stomach growled even thinking about food.

"The dog don't have a name. That's the Corporal." The Yank quickly extended his hand towards Bill. "Welcome to the Ambulance Field Service. Higgins, is it?"

The Yank waited for Bill's nod. "I'm Mikey Doyle. I volunteered to work with the American Ambulance Hospital in Neuilly, and I ended up driving this here motor ambulance. What about you?"

Bill felt a bit uncertain. Only a few hours before, he had been plucked from his friends and comrades in the trenches. His pals. Then his trusted sergeant had abandoned him with no clear orders, and now this 'Yank', as Keane had called him, was grinning at him just like the Cheshire cat drawing in Alice's Adventures in Wonderland. He should be worried, but instead, Bill felt an instinctive warmth towards Mikey Doyle.

"My friends call me Bill," Bill replied. "I'm from near Windsor."

"Like the King, eh?" The Yank winked. "Well, Bill, let's get going then." Doyle had one of those homely faces, wavy dark hair, wide green eyes, and an easy-going grin. "And you call me Mikey or call me Yank if you want. I don't give a shit."

The language made Bill feel more at ease. He grinned and allowed his tense shoulders to relax somewhat.

Bill stared at the dog again. It seemed strange that he didn't have a name. *Did it ever have a name?* he wondered. The dog cocked his head as if he knew exactly what Bill was thinking. *Sam, it looked like a Sam to him.*

"Any idea what I'm going to be doing, Mikey?" It felt wrong to call him Yank. Bill's knee was juddering, and he was anxious to find out any information he could and was sure this American might have an idea. And he wasn't wrong.

"Sure thing." Mikey pointed downward to the dog curled up between them. "You've already met the Corporal. He's a dog of war but on the medical rescue side, mainly. He's your assignment."

At the mention of his name, the Corporal looked up even more intently at Bill. His eyes had not left him since Bill had entered the ambulance. Bill felt another pang of homesickness. The Corporal seemed to sense this and woofed at him.

Bill and Mikey laughed together, and the young English soldier stretched out his right hand and stroked the Corporal's head with real affection.

Bill still felt confused. He was no medic.

"You men! Get that damn contraption out of here!" The orders came from a man on a horse who was directing men, carts and wagons out of the forward supply area.

"God damned Military Mounted Police," growled Mikey doing a mock salute behind the man's back.

Mikey waved at the horseman, and the motorised ambulance lurched forward in a loud clatter, belching more acrid smoke.

Bill could feel every pothole and rut, and he held on for dear life, his face visibly drained of blood.

The Corporal woofed at him again and laid his head on Bill's right leg as if to reassure him. Mikey noticed this and clapped Bill on the shoulder in a friendly fashion.

"Looks like the Corporal likes you, and that's a good thing." They were on a smoother section of the road now. The noise of the motor wasn't as loud, and the muddy landscape was changing rapidly to green countryside and hedgerows. They had gone from war-torn landscape to peace in just a few miles. It was France but another France, another world away.

"What do you mean he's my assignment?"

"Well, you, my new pal, Bill, will have the honour of bodyguarding the Corporal here."

Mikey chuckled at the look of confusion on Bill's face. It wasn't the first time the American had seen that look. He only hoped Bill would be the last bodyguard, but he had his doubts. The life expectancy of a medic and message carrier dog like the Corporal was normally a short one. However, the Corporal had saved some Colonel's life and now had a permanent bodyguard assigned to him: an especially dangerous assignment on the battlefield as the German snipers liked to target these dogs.

"Don't fret, Bill; all will be revealed when we get to the hospital area." Mikey smiled, but his eyes didn't follow his lips. Mikey didn't have the heart to elaborate. He'd leave that to others. Being assigned as a bodyguard to the Corporal was tantamount to a death sentence, or so it had been for the three previous soldiers before Bill.

It was a shame. The boy seemed like a real nice kid. But then so had the others.

It didn't pay to get attached to nobody in this job. *His new pal, Bill.* Mikey carried on staring straight ahead. Shit, it was cold.

2.
PROMOTION

THE NEXT FEW WEEKS were filled with training alongside Corporal getting to know the role of a medic and messenger dog on the battlefield. Bill was told everything he needed to know apart from his life expectancy. He didn't need to know that. None of them did.

Bill was left stunned at times at the sheer intelligence that Corporal displayed. The Airedale wasn't a particularly handsome species of dog with its flat forehead and wiry coat, but Corporal made up for that in sheer size and weight. He was an impressive 30 inches tall at the shoulder and weighed in at a muscle-rippling 80 pounds.

Bill suspected Corporal was a crossbreed and not a pure terrier. He was certainly twice the size of John's dog

Pip. Corporal had a regal look about him, especially with his long muscular legs. Above all, it was the eyes. Corporal's eyes shone with smarts, and at times, Bill even expected him to start talking.

Nobody knew Corporal's true origins. They said he had been found limping and frightened in No Man's Land. Most likely, he had been a working dog from a nearby farm and got lost, or perhaps he was a soldier's pet or a war dog. If he was German, he didn't show it. There was no way he was German, decided Bill.

Whatever breed he was, Bill and Corporal quickly became inseparable. They slept in the same tent, ate together, and when it came to washing, Bill had to scrub Corporal first before he could even begin on himself. Well, Corporal was a corporal after all and Bill a mere private.

"Where's your shadow, mate?" yelled every soldier if ever Bill was seen alone, even for one second.

Corporal particularly liked being groomed with the horse currycomb they had acquired from the nearby Mounted Military Police stables. If the truth be known, Bill had just trailed behind Corporal, who slipped into the stables unnoticed by crawling in slowly on his belly. He'd disappeared among the bales of hay, snorting horses and piles of manure, then come trotting back minutes later with the currycomb in his mouth. Very pleased with himself, he had a particularly mischievous look in his eyes as if to say, "What about that then!"

They'd been in an instant bond between the pair, but Bill had realised even more that Corporal was very special. He was no ordinary dog for sure. From that day, an unbreakable bond was forged between bodyguard and dog. The young soldier had come to trust Corporal's instincts too. He learned to trust his body language, and trust his experience of war as Bill had none yet, not yet having seen any action. The Corporal seemed to know well ahead of any soldier: his alert, pricked up ears, his uncanny senses, his low growl all preceded distant bombardments.

The two spent days and nights playing hide and seek through the nearby woods as the primroses poked their way up through the frozen earth. Bill learned to recognise Corporal's footprints and how to follow his trail. Corporal revelled in jumping out at Bill and scaring him half to death during their night excursions.

Bill also came to understand Corporal's different woofs and barks. In a way, the Airedale did talk. Not human talk, of course, but he made himself clearly understood, at least to Bill he did.

During this time, Bill got to know Mikey Doyle, the motorised ambulance driver. Mikey was ten years older than Bill, but the American had an openness about him and such an honest sense of humour that Bill could not help liking this brash companion. They spent many evenings outside Bill's tent getting to know each other. Corporal curled up, watching the two chat and woofing as if joining the conversation so neither of them would forget he was there.

Mikey was from a small town in a place called the Commonwealth of Pennsylvania in the United States, and he was a true patriot. He had travelled to France at the outbreak of war with Germany to assist the nation that had helped his country during the War of Independence. Bill knew nothing about American history and was quite surprised to discover the war in the late 1770s had been against England.

Mikey, on the other hand, was also a self-confessed romantic and had been quite taken aback to have been rebuffed by the *L'Armée de Terre*, the French Army. Nevertheless, he was still determined to do his bit. When Mikey heard the US Ambassador Myron Herrick was setting up the American Ambulance Hospital to treat wounded French soldiers, he had signed up for the duration.

"America might be a neutral country, Bill, but many of us 'Yanks' feel an affinity with France and even Britain. You'd be surprised how many Irish, Scots and English people are now in the States."

"Tell me, though, Mikey, why do people call you lot Yanks?"

Bill was genuinely interested, and Mikey admitted he wasn't quite sure, except it was a term used during the civil war and by many foreigners. All Bill took away from this conversation was that he had a lot to learn about America. He had a lot to learn about many things. Even though the Berkshire Pals Battalion had been in France for some months now, they had never been in battle.

Sergeant Keane had visited him regularly in the first weeks. The first time he brought the rest of Bill's kit and news of the platoon. John was doing well, and that pleased the young soldier greatly. On the Sergeant's last visit, he had introduced Bill to a dour red-headed and red-faced Scotsman dressed in a tartan kilt with a knife sticking out of his left boot.

Bill wondered if every sergeant was red-faced by default. It probably came of all the burst blood vessels from shouting, he thought.

"Staff Sergeant McTaggart is an expert in hand-to-hand combat, Private Higgins." Keane was unblinking, all business as usual. "He has agreed to teach you how to fight at close quarters and how to stay alive and how to use that rifle of yours to best effect. He's doing so as a personal favour to me, so you pay heed to him, you hear?"

Sergeant James McTaggart was short but barrel-chested with thick muscled arms and legs like tree trunks. His entire body was covered in thick curly red hair, and he evoked real fear in Bill. There was no doubt in the young soldier's mind that this man was brutal. Corporal seemed also weary of the wild Scotsman. He sat on his haunches, watching and letting out low growls every time Bill trained with the staff sergeant. And McTaggart was a hard taskmaster.

They trained every day, but Sunday and most nights, Bill crawled into his tent, black and blue all over. A bloody nose or black eye swollen shut were common results of their bouts of unarmed combat. Sargeant McTaggart was an irresistible force, but Bill was learning with every cut and bruise. His young body was also gaining muscle thanks to a good diet and hard exercise.

Day after day, the Scotsman from the 1st Battalion of the Royal Scots Regiment put Bill through his paces. A five-mile run with Corporal at dawn followed by breakfast, then to the rifle range for the rest of the morning followed by unarmed combat training in the afternoon. There was no lunch, just water and hard biscuits. Sundays were the only days of respite from the mad Scotsman's relentless training regime.

On that day of rest, Bill noticed McTaggart always visited one nurse at the field hospital. Nurse Abigail Edgefield was a wonder to behold and was particularly fond of the young English soldier. From a 'good' English family, posh but not in your face with it, she had a classic English rose beauty that reminded Bill of the actress, Gabriella Ray, whose beautiful face and form graced numerous postcards in the village shop back in Sunnington Down.

If there was any romance between her and the Scotsman, Nurse Abigail gave no sign of it.

"You tell me if that Scots brute hurts you too much, Bill." Sister Edgefield said in a motherly way while patching him up after a singularly hard round of training. "And you, Corporal, how can you let Bill get into such a shocking state?"

She tutted, and Bill looked on quite astonished as Corporal sank to his haunches and, obviously very aware of Nurse Abigail's displeasure for not protecting him, slinked out of the medical tent looking decidedly guilty. It made Bill laugh with much merriment but not for long, as it hurt. When he asked about the Staff Sergeant, Nurse Abigail shook her head.

"Jim is a product of your British Army and spending many years in India," was all she revealed.

Bill never pressed her again but found it interesting that both Sargeant Keane and McTaggart had served in India.

Bill was wondering more about both men's time in India one afternoon while queuing at the mess tent for tea, when a particularly savage blow to his stomach felled Bill like a tree, leaving him winded and gasping for breath, pain exploding up through his chest and down to his groin.

"Pay attention, laddie." McTaggart now loomed over him with a grim look on his face. "Dinnae ever let yeer attention wander or yee'll likely as not end up deed or worse, yee'll get Corporal there killt and if that 'appens, yee'll find yeeself in front of a firing squad."

McTaggart was right, of course. He had been momentarily daydreaming and deserved to be punished for it.

As Bill lay on the ground clutching himself in pain, and gasping for breath, Corporal started barking and snarling at McTaggart and then advanced menacingly on the staff sergeant.

There was no doubt that Corporal meant business and was about to attack.

"Corporal, no!" Bill gasped, managing to make himself heard despite his badly-winded state.

Corporal stopped on command and looked at Bill and then back at McTaggart with jowls pulled back, teeth bared.

Slowly, Corporal backed away but didn't take his eyes off the Scotsman, and McTaggart remained very still, frozen to the spot. But surprisingly, the Staff Sergeant was grinning at Bill.

Bill pulled himself up to sitting and winced.

"Yee've got a reel comrade there, Bill." It was the first time McTaggart had ever called him Bill, and Bill had no idea of what to make of that as he raised himself off the ground.

"I've noo seen him like that with any of his other minders afore."

Bill was about to ask him how many other minders the Corporal had had and then thought better of it. "I think we'll call it a day, yee've learned aboot as much as I ken teach ye. Me battalion's back in the trenches in a few days, and I have got a lot tae do. Aye, so I have."

The Scotsman nodded, his clear blue eyes grave for a moment as they wished the young soldier bonne chance. He saluted Bill; then his eyes twinkled as they darted over towards the tented hospital area. 'A lot to do' meant his romancing of the Gabrielle Ray lookalike, Bill guessed.

With that, McTaggart turned and walked back towards the tented hospital area. No doubt to pay his respects to Nurse Abigail, thought Bill.

Bill knew he had been honoured with these one-on-one lessons, but they weren't on his account, they were on the Corporal's. He was a nothing.

He'd only just got up to standing when he spotted Sergeant Keane walking towards him with a haversack slung over his left shoulder.

"I saw that, Private Higgins. Hurt, did it?" Keane spoke fast as he approached, without a smile, unslinging the haversack as he did so.

Bill expected the two red-faced sergeants to exchange greetings, but they did not as they walked past each other as if neither existed, which was strange. They were friends, after all.

Bill pushed the thought to the back of his mind and turned to Keane.

"Sarge! What brings you here today?" Bill asked in genuine interest.

He couldn't help but stare at the haversack as it seemed to have some importance to this meeting.

"You're looking well, Bill." That was the second time a Sergeant had used his nickname in a matter of minutes. It made Bill uneasy, and Corporal came trotting up and sat next to him. He, too, could sense a change in the air and wanted to be close to Bill.

"Walk with me, lad," Keane spoke in a tone reminiscent of his father Joseph when he was explaining the facts of life to a somewhat embarrassed Bill. "Your assignment to protect Corporal comes from way up the chain of command. This dog is very important to someone, and word has just come down to me that a Private doesn't have the rank to do the job."

Bill stopped dead in his tracks. He must have heard wrong. After all the weeks of training with Corporal, enduring the so-called 'instruction' in weapons and close-quarters combat by that maniacal Scotsman? Now some rear echelon paper-pusher was sending him back to the platoon. Without Corporal. That wasn't fair on either of them.

Bill shot a glance of panic to Corporal and was about to express his dismay when Keane help up his hand to silence him.

"It's not what you think."

Keane threw the haversack to Bill. It was heavy and felt like it contained some sort of tools. Bill weighed it in his hands.

From his left tunic pocket, the Sergeant pulled out a cloth with the stripes of a non-commissioned officer and held it out. "You are Sergeant Bill Higgins now, Bill. You are on detached service from the Berkshire Pals, and it is very unlikely we'll meet again."

There was no time for emotion and for the reality of the Sarge's words to sink in as the Sarge reached into his pocket and pulled out a folded letter.

"I have your written orders here, and in that haversack, you'll find some useful equipment."

Bill took the sergeant's stripes and the folded letter of orders. He opened and closed his mouth a few times and was clearly at a loss for words. In fact, he was totally confused, and he couldn't think properly.

Corporal jumped up with his front paws and woofed at him as he saluted the Sarge.

Bill looked down at Corporal and stroked his curly head. At least he and the Corporal weren't being parted. That's all he could think of right now. The relief was immediate.

By the time he looked back up and away from Corporal, Keane had left and was walking off in the same direction McTaggart had taken.

He was now a sergeant, unbelievable! Bill hunched down with Corporal and was about to go through the haversack. Then it struck him. The explanation for this extraordinary turn of events would not be in the haversack but in his written orders.

Bill unfolded the thick paper which would reveal his future and began to read.

***

McTaggart watched grimly as Keane approached him. He held out a silver flask to the Sergeant, who nodded and took a long slug of the whisky inside.

"He's a good 'un, Albert." McTaggart said it like he meant it. He could tell his friend was fond of the lad, and that wasn't good in times of war and with what the boy was about to face. "He's a crack shot with a rifle and revolver, and I'd be happy to have him with me in any kind of fight."

Gone was any trace of a Scottish brogue. McTaggart spoke in clear accent-less military English, addressing Keane as only brothers-in-arms who had seen action together could, with feeling and an understanding of the strength of the bond between them.

"I would feel better if he was permanently assigned to ambulance service, but according to his orders, he will also be required to conduct special duties."

Keane looked his friend right in the face. Both men knew what that meant. They, too, during their long careers with the army, had been on 'special duties'. It had been on one such bloody assignment that they had first met.

"Nothing to be done about that, Sergeant Keane." McTaggart snapped harshly. "Get your shiite together. Yee've have a whole company of men to command, so you have."

Keane nodded and glanced back at the new Sergeant Higgins squatting in the grass on the side of the hill with his dog.

Good luck to you, Bill, lad, you are going to need it, Keane said silently to himself before turning and walking away.

McTaggart watched him go and took a last swig from his silver flask. The liquid burned its way down his throat and warmed his stomach. There was one last gesture of confidence he had to make before heading back to the battalion.

3.
MINERS

"LISTEN CLOSELY, SERGEANT." Captain Archibald Wootton of the Royal Engineers looked exhausted. The men of his Tunnelling Companies had been working towards the German lines for months, and conditions were bad, to say the least.

The threat of constant cave-ins, cramped conditions and drunkenness among the miners plagued progress. The previous year, on this same front in Flanders, German pioneers had tunnelled under no man's land and exploded a 120-pound mine below the trenches of the Indian Sirhind Brigade covering the Givenchy-lès-la-Bassée area. The Huns quickly launched a surprise attack on the stunned and confused Indians, and a whole company of 800 soldiers was wiped out in the ensuing fighting. It was an awakening to an aspect of this war that stunned the Generals of the British High Command.

At this stage of the conflict, it was a stalemate. Trenches on both sides of no man's land now bristled with machinegun nests and barbed wire, making it suicide for frontal attacking infantry. So this aspect of warfare should have come as no surprise as tunnelling and blowing up fortifications had been standard practice among armies since the 15th century.

"One of the new shafts has collapsed 90-feet underground on level two, and we need to find out if anyone is still alive down there."

Wootton had to speak up as he explained the mission to the young Sergeant standing before him. His voice was clipped, speaking of a schooling somewhere like Harrow or Eton too. But he had less of a sneer than most captains that Bill met. Maybe it was the exhaustion setting in: he had no energy to act like the Lord of the Manor here. Or maybe it was his age: he looked in his late 30s.

Bill strained his ears. The noise of bellowing NCOs, neighing horses, and the general clamour of soldiers at work shifting, stacking, unloading, and distributing supplies, food and water made for the usual military racket in the background.

The captain pointed his finger at a hand-drawn map of the tunnel network to indicate where level two was located. On paper, the tunnels branched out in all directions and looked like the outline of a game of Snakes and Ladders with numbers marking levels and shaft depths and lengths clearly visible.

Bill fought against a rising feeling of sheer horror at the thought of descending into this maze of excavations. He managed to keep his nerves under control and any sign of panic off his face.

Corporal sat straight up with his body directly over his hips next to Bill as the Captain laid out the details of the rescue operation. He sensed the unease in his trusted friend and recognised the faint whiff of fear in the air. It was nothing new to Corporal, and he nudged Bill's left leg with his head to remind him they were in this together. The movement caught the eye of the Captain of Engineers.

"So this is the famous Corporal I've heard so much about." Captain Wootton looked down at the dog whose head cleared table height. "Big bugger for an Airedale, isn't he?"

"Smart too, sir." Bill was somewhat surprised at how steady his voice was. There was no outward indication of the turmoil that gripped him, and to express his pride in Corporal was a welcome distraction. "If anyone can get this job done, it's Corporal here."

Wootton noticed the Sergeant's use of "anyone" to describe the dog as if the animal was human or perhaps even superhuman. The two were certainly close. That was obvious to anyone who understood what 'man's best friend' meant in real terms. And Wootton understood perfectly. He knew of the many dog mascots to be found in the trenches. Think of a breed, and you'd probably find one in the front lines. These animals provided companionship to the ordinary soldiers and were loved by the men for keeping the trenches clear of the rats that plagued every miserable muddy corner. They were a real morale booster for men living in less-than-ideal condition, worth every scrap of food the starving soldiers salvaged for them. The French Army even used canines to pull heavy machine guns and ammunition to the front.

The British High Command had recently made it an offence punishable by Court Martial for soldiers to own any number of breeds of dog. Just like horses used to pull wagons and artillery, dogs were now an integral part of the war machine on the Western Front. They were no longer pets; they were soldiers.

"In normal circumstances, Sergeant Higgins, I would not ask you to do this. However, it is imperative for the men's morale right now that the miners know the Corps of Engineers will attempt a rescue when things go wrong." Wootton rubbed his stubbled chin and looked up at the NCO standing before him.

The Sergeant was young, probably in his teens, but then the trenches were filled with so many soldiers about his age these days. Still, the Captain didn't envy the young soldier the task before him. He was equally relieved it wasn't himself going down into those ghastly tunnels.

A wave of sickening guilt washed over Wootton momentarily as he realised he could be sending this young man to his death. His own son was about the same age but was still studying at Eton, thankfully.

"Go with Mr Willard, Sergeant, and jolly good luck." The Captain dismissed Bill and Corporal with a wave of his hand in the direction of an older man standing just off to the right of the table.

Mr Willard removed a smoking pipe from his mouth and stood up. He gestured with his iron-grey head for them to follow him outside the command tent.

The organised army chaos was still in full swing when they emerged into the sunlight. Soldiers were on the move in every direction, many carrying petrol cans full of water to slake the thirst of their comrades in the nearby trenches. The smell of cooking was everywhere as the field kitchens prepared to feed thousands of hungry men. At least it wasn't raining. The sky was a clear blue, and the spring sunshine exuded warmth and lifted everyone's spirits.

The daffodils seemed strangely out of place here, but here they were nonetheless, here defiant among all the mud.

Much to Bill's astonishment, Mr Willard was dressed in civilian clothes. Heavy boots, grey trousers and a tweed jacket were a clear statement that he was not in the army. He was an older man in his 50s, squat in stature with a square moustache under his nose, all the rage these days. His grey eyes had that washed-out look that came with age and hard experiences. A strong jaw, hawk-like nose and well-worn face indicated a man used to being obeyed.

As they shook hands, Bill could feel the callouses that marked Willard as a man of action rather than an 'office wallah' as Sergeant Keane used to call the Battalion's clerks. An expression that Keane had picked up in India and often used in contempt of those he considered soft, lily-livered and weak-willed.

"I will be sending you down with one of my best men." Willard motioned to a rather willowy figure sitting atop of boxes clearly marked 'Explosives'. He was also smoking a pipe.

Briefly, Bill wondered if all tunnellers smoke pipes. This was the first time he had met any miners as his home county of Berkshire was mainly agricultural with a scattering of breweries. Perhaps smoking tobacco in a pipe was a sign of the working-class. He'd not seen many officers using them.

"Allan, come over and meet Sergeant Higgins and his mercy dog," Willard called the willowy man over.

Allan Dyson was a Nottinghamshire miner who had been down the coal mines since he was fourteen. In thirty years, he had experienced everything underground mining could throw at a man. Rockfalls, crushed limbs, men dead of suffocation due to no oxygen at deep levels. He'd even survived lethal explosions of pockets of methane gas twice.

Dyson had been among the first miners to volunteer for one of the eight Tunnelling Companies formed in the February of 1915. Within a week, he was in Flanders hard at work as a Royal Engineer sapper. No basic training, no rifle drills or marching; these men weren't meant for the trenches. They were highly skilled, and their job was to carve out tunnels to intercept and destroy the Hun pioneers tunnelling from the opposite side.

"For King and Country, eh, Sergeant Higgins?" Dyson didn't offer to shake hands. Instead, he looked Bill up and down and then spat on the ground.

A single bark saturated with menace rang out. Corporal stood stiff, the hair along his back raised as was his tail. His ears lay flat along the side of his head. He snarled at the newcomer, and there was no mistaking the dog's intent.

Corporal did not move; he did not have to. Dyson held up his hands in a gesture of surrender, clearly shaken and fearful.

"Hell, Sergeant, get your animal under control." Willard had also stepped away in shock, and Bill had to admit Corporal's posture was wild and dangerous and full of menace.

Good boy, he thought to himself. Served the miner right for insulting them.

"With respect, Corporal is not 'my animal', Mr Willard." Everyone they came across just assumed Bill was Corporal's handler, and this was far from the truth. "Corporal holds a non-commissioned officer rank in the British Army. My orders are to keep Corporal safe at all times, even if it means taking a bullet for him."

Bill paused. He adored the dog. Take a bullet for him he would without a moment's hesitation. It wasn't about orders anymore. It was about love. The bond a man can form with an animal that went deeper than any of the bloody tunnels they were about to bury under.

"It is Corporal who is given assignments, and I tag along to assist in any way I can. That is my duty, Mr Willard."

"It looks like Corporal is equally determined to keep you just as safe, Sergeant." Dyson let out a short nervous laugh which lowered the tension considerably.

Corporal visibly relaxed. He stepped forward, cocked his leg, and urinated on the ground just in front of the two miners.

"Upon my soul!" Willard gasped. Neither he nor Dyson had seen the likes of such a dog before. "If I am not mistaken, Allan, this dog has just pissed on us!"

"Aye, I think you're right, by God!" Dyson and Willard laughed aloud, and Bill could not help joining in.

Corporal gave a friendly woof, and the laughter rose above the general din, drawing odd looks from the men working nearby.

"I can certainly work with the Sergeant and Corporal. Aye, they are certainly made of the right stuff.' Dyson nodded. "Come on, Corporal, let's go to the tunnel entrance and bring that Sergeant Higgins of yours with you."

Dyson grinned as he turned away and strode off in long strides.

The whiff of his pipe smoke lingered in the spot he'd been standing moments before. Corporal looked at Bill for permission, and Bill nodded, *let's go*.

"Good luck to the both of you, and I sincerely hope that this mission is not in vain." Mr Willard's parting words rang in Bill's ears as he followed Dyson and Corporal through the throng of soldiers towards the tunnel entrance.

When they arrived, Bill looked about him in confusion. There were three square walls of sandbags spaced out and a number of wooden winches atop of them from which men were drawing out buckets of water. So they were wells, but where was the tunnel entrance?

"Get yourselves ready now.' Dyson nodded grimly. "We will start down in a few minutes. I just have to make some arrangements so we can lower Corporal down safely."

Dyson was all business now, and he went off shouting out a number of names and a stream of instructions.

Bill squatted down next to Corporal, and then out of his knapsack, he pulled a pair of canvas bags attached together by leather straps. This was a first-aid kit adapted from the cavalry. Each bag contained a small scissors, sterile gauze, bandages, antiseptic sponges, sterile dressings, and sutures.

A third pouch which was positioned on Corporal's back between his front shoulders, contained a flask of water. This was the Mercy Dog gear that Corporal used when scouring the battlefield for wounded and dying soldiers. He was also trained to lead stretcher-bearers to hard-to-find living wounded among hundreds and most often thousands of dead strewn among the carnage.

"You ready for this, boy?" Bill asked Corporal, who then licked his face with enthusiasm.

Corporal was in his element. This is what he was trained for, what he excelled at. All Bill had to do was follow Corporal's lead and get him back to safety. The only thing was, no one had told him about going nearly 100-foot underground in a tunnel complex which had already collapsed and had trapped a number of miners. But it was not his place to question, it was his place to do.

From inside his tunic, Bill pulled out a silver flask. It has been a parting gift from Staff Sergeant McTaggart. He took a long gulp and felt whisky burn all the way to his belly. Fortified with Dutch courage, Bill got to his feet and replaced the flask into his tunic.

Miners and soldiers had by now gathered all about them. The word had gone out that the rescue team was here and about to descend into the tunnel network.

Shouts of 'good luck' and 'bring 'em back' rang out. Bill looked at the sea of faces about him. Most were grimy from digging as the tunnelling work continued despite the cave-in. The war stopped for no man.

"We're ready, Mr Dyson," Bill said with as much confidence he could muster.

"We've attached a basket for Corporal and will lower him down using the winch while you follow me down the ladder," Dyson replied, pointing to one of the wooden winches which moments before was being used to draw water. "Let's get this show on the road and pray to the almighty that nothing goes wrong, Sergeant."

Bill had not been feeling so nervous before. Now a feeling of cold dread seized his insides and wouldn't let him go.

Bill looked at Corporal, and for a moment, he could have sworn he saw the dog wink at him.

4.
THE TUNNEL

THE SHAFT LEADING TO THE TUNNEL NETWORK had been sunk vertically into the earth and was little more than four feet square. Its walls were clad all the way to the bottom with carefully crafted and fitted wood slats. According to Lance Corporal Allan Dyson, whose role was as a shift boss, the slats were to prevent the natural ground pressure from collapsing access and the miners' only way back to the surface.

The main shaft was cramped, and Bill soon stopped looking up as the sky above had seemed to shrink as he climbed down the ladder after Dyson.

It got colder the further they went down. After five minutes, Corporal and Bill made it to the first level of the tunnel network without trouble.

Corporal dangled from a rope attached to his harness for a moment until Bill pulled him onto the platform and untied him. The shaft itself continued on down into the blackness.

"You okay, boy?" Bill ruffled the dog's head. Corporal gave Bill a soft whoof and stepped into the tunnel ahead where Dyson awaited them.

What little light there was down here came from candles, of all things anchored to tiny shelves cut into the walls at ten feet intervals. To Bill, the orange glow cast by the candlelight was beautiful yet somehow disturbing as shadows of men, and dark niches in the roughly hewn chalk rock flickered the length of the receding tunnel.

The scene was one of the men moving quietly down the tunnel, others standing to the side of walls as a small wooden trolley full of rock and mining debris was pushed towards the entrance on a pair of railway tracks.

There seemed to be virtually no room for trolly and man to pass each other in the same space, but they did, much to Bill's amazement.

"The trolly wheels are made of rubber to keep the noise down." The Lance Corporal explained in hushed tones when he noticed Bill's interest. "We have to work in near silence down here or face the Hun hearing us and setting off a mine charge. Every day, my men face being entombed, downed, or gassed by carbon monoxide."

Dyson paused, candlelight flickering on his grim face. He counted off on his hands. "In the last four weeks alone, we've had 38 men hospitalised, another 57 minor injuries we could treat here at the shaft head, and

16 men killed. It's just too much, which is why you're here now."

These workings were a seriously dangerous place to be, and Dyson's revelations did little to calm Bill's nerves. In fact, they had the opposite effect. The cold that had gripped him at the entrance still had him in its vice-like grip.

They moved forward, and the wood-lined walls of the main shaft were replaced with thick wood props shoring up the sides and roof at regular intervals.

Bill felt a steady flow of air coming from within the tunnel network ruffling his hair in the process. He was about to ask how this was possible when Dyson forestalled his question.

"Don't ask me to explain the technicalities, but we have two other shafts sunk into the network, and they help circulate fresh air. We've also got bellows at the top for a backup at deeper levels." The Lance Corporal seemed very much in his element as he pointed to air pipes running along the walls.

Dyson coughed. A raspy miner's cough. "At the bottom of each shaft is a pump for draining the tunnels and gathering water to slake the thirst of thousands of you soldiers. Water is drawn twice a day, morning and evening, in between the winders hoist out the spoil."

Dyson led off with Bill and Corporal hot on his heels. Neither of them wanted to be in this netherworld any longer than they had to, and the safest place to be seemed to be as close as possible to the Lance Corporal.

With each step, the young Sergeant could feel the urge rising in him to run back the way they had come. It was only by a conscious effort that he managed to keep control. The tunnel walls were closing in on him, and the atmosphere seemed to be getting colder and wetter. Despite this, sweat ran freely inside his clothing.

They had covered about 100 feet when Dyson turned into another section branching off to the left. At first glance, it looked like an enlarged grotto, perhaps a resting place. On closer inspection, Bill could see the frame of a winch or winder, as Dyson called it, along with a thick rope disappearing into a large black hole. The top of a ladder protruded. Under his boots, he could feel the railway tracks for the wooden trollies the miners used to remove rock and debris back to the surface.

"This shaft will take us directly to the entrance of the level where we had the rockfall," Dyson spoke in a soft, matter-of-fact manner as he casually secured the rope to the top of Corporal's harness. "Get yourself down the ladder, Sergeant, and I will lower Corporal down to you."

Peering into the square hole, Bill could only just see the light flickering dimly at the bottom, albeit very dimly. It was eerily quiet in the tunnel despite the many men at work.

Steeling himself and taking a deep breath, Bill slipped beneath the winch and found a rung on the ladder with his left boot. He wavered just a moment and then descended very carefully into the void.

He fought the urge to scream as this would lead to uncontrollable panic, Bill knew. But it was a close-run thing until he felt Corporal's rear leg paws brush the top of his head. For some inexplicable reason, he found the contact reassuring, and it steadied his nerves. Just knowing Corporal was there with him speeded up the final 20 feet of groping his way down the ladder.

"You the rescue team? I'm Rick Tyler, pleased to help in any way I can," whispered a dark figure crouched a few feet into the next tunnel.

Bill ignored the man and turned instead to grasp Corporal as he was lowered down the last few feet. Tail wagging, Corporal licked Bill's face. So he, too, was glad that was over. At least next time they would be heading out of this coffin-like pit, sighed Bill.

As Bill untied the rope, Dyson's boots slipped into view. Thanks to a pair of heavy leather gloves and years of working underground, he had slid down the ladder rather than use the rungs.

Corporal and Bill moved to one side in the cramped space as the Lance Corporal joined them down there. Cramped was not really an accurate description. The space was terrifyingly claustrophobic, with rock above and below and on each side of a tiny crawlspace 100 feet below the surface.

There must be thousands of tons of rock above them. The very thought made Bill shiver, and in doing so, he bashed the top of his head on the rock ceiling. He must have hit a jagged piece of rock as the pain was instant and fierce, and for a brief moment, Bill thought he might pass out.

He stifled any cry of pain from the injury and instead reached out to stroke Corporal's head to reassure himself. Corporal felt so warm, so comforting, so his.

"Come on; we've lost enough time as it is. Out the way there, Wilson." Dyson addressed the crouched figure hidden in the shadows of the flickering candlelight. "This is the promised rescue team."

As they moved through the dimly-lit crawl space, roughly hewn rock streaked black in places by greasy candle smoke, the more Bill found he had to crouch lower and lower. The descent towards the scene of the rock face collapse was definitely narrowing considerably.

It wasn't long before Dyson stopped and motioned to the jumble of rocks to his front. To one side, a single candle had been placed in a nook, and the flame wavered as if struggling to stay lit. If the candle went out, then it meant there was zero oxygen left in the tunnel, and evacuation had to be fast.

Dyson had briefed Bill on what to expect during their journey, but now the young Sergeant faced the actual fact he could feel himself shaking. He had to control his fear of this place, its confines, and the fact that somewhere in front of them were the crushed remains of two men. Two husbands, fathers, brothers, and sons. Mates like John.

"Right, we've seen the cave-in, now let's get out of here and fast," Dyson squeezed past Bill and started to double back the way they had come. His sudden reaction was unexpected, and the young Sergeant looked after the retreating Lance Corporal with some confusion.

"They are both dead, Sergeant." Dyson stopped and turned when he realised they were not following him. "We had to show a willingness to attempt a rescue, and we have. Now let's get back."

Just then, Corporal started pawing at the shattered boulders and assorted rock debris.

The Airedale was working himself into a frenzy and started barking in a muted kind of way as if understanding he too had to be quiet down here.

He looked back at Bill, and his ears went flat alongside his head. It was Corporal's way of saying, 'don't ignore me if you know what's good for you'.

"Get back here, Dyson, and bring extra men. Now!" Bill was suddenly in charge and reached over Corporal and started removing rocks from the pile. "You get back now, boy; there's not enough room for both of us."

As Corporal retreated, other men came up beside Bill. Soon a chain of men passed rock after rock back along the tunnel.

The air was turning putrid fast, and the candle went out. It was relit and went out again and was lit once more.

The smell of sweat and fear lay heavy on the men, but nobody made a move to leave the cramped tunnel.

"How long have they been trapped down here?" Bill asked the man next to him.

"Three hours or so now. It's hard to tell, but they are probably goners anyway, poor sods." The man used a bandana to wipe the dirt and sweat from his face. The candlelight gave them all a ghoulish look in such a confined space.

Bill kept on pulling at the rocks in front of him and passing them back. The work went on and on, time seemed now of no importance, just the rhythmic passing of rock from man to man.

Bill found himself somewhat hypnotised by the repetition, but he felt himself growing weaker by the second and colder too. Water must be dripping from the ceiling as the young Sergeant felt it running down his head and neck in a steady stream. But then he realised with a sickening feeling it must be blood from his wound.

He grabbed another rock, his hands now cut and bloody, and he pulled at it. Much to his annoyance, it did not move. Bill stared at the boot he had firmly in his grasp. For a moment, he did not realise what he was looking at. Then it hit him, and he crawled back and out of the way towards where Corporal lay silent and watching.

"Quick. You men get those rocks off him."

Bill called out to Corporal, and his companion shot through the line of men.

The miners soon exposed the body, and they gently slid it out of the rubble, half expecting another cave-in. Then the corpse coughed and gasped.

Shocked men nearly let him drop to the tunnel floor. But Corporal shot forward and started licking the man's face, reviving the man still further.

Bill removed the flask containing water from Corporal's back and then lifted the man's head up and carefully dribbled the liquid over his mouth and face.

A deep gash in the miner's forehead and a torn ear bled profusely in a spreading stain. There seemed to be an awful lot of blood everywhere. Bill realised it was collecting and mingling with his own.

"You men," Bill addressed the chain of miners who had kept up the relentless human conveyor. "Pass this chap down to the end and do it gently now. Corporal and I will follow. Careful, he's got some bad cuts, and we don't know what internal injuries."

The miners handed their wounded comrade from man to man with a tenderness Bill had not expected from such a rough and tough bunch. They made room for the Sergeant and Corporal as they followed closely. It was hard and slow going, and when they reached the bottom of the ladder leading to level one, Bill turned to the man crouched there.

"Tyler, isn't it?" It was not a question but more of a statement of fact. "Get up to the surface, and you will find a motorised ambulance nearby. The chap in there is a medic called Doyle. Tell him we have a survivor coming up."

"Right you are, gov." Tyler raised his knuckle to his forehead in the English workman's traditional way of taking orders from a superior.

The salute-like gesture surprised Bill, but he had little time for that now. He pulled a medic pack from one of the Corporal's canvas bags and pulled out an antiseptic sponge. Bill quickly cleaned the area around the gash and the torn ear and applied sterile dressing before swathing the injured man's head in a bandage.

"Get him tied to the rope under the arms and get him to the surface. As fast as you can, lads." Bill, with Corporal in tow, headed back to the scene of the cave-in, adrenaline speeding his weary and cold limbs. If there was any chance the second man was also alive, he had to be there.

Just then, Bill realised he was free of any form of fear, having been caught up in saving a life with Corporal leading the way.

Halfway back along the tunnel, Bill and Corporal stopped. They could now see the second cave-in victim being manhandled gently down the line. There were no smiles this time, just grim faces.

Bill's heart sank, and any elation he had felt at the rescue disappeared. Death, death, and more death. Is this all he could expect as a future?

Bill sat back on the tunnel floor and dropped his head down. He was exhausted physically and mentally.

"Corporal, go to the ladder. There's a good chap. I'll follow shortly." Bill did not want his beloved companion to see him fall apart, and he signalled for the canny Airedale to be on his way.

Corporal woofed at him and licked his face, and refused to budge. He did not seem to mind the taste of blood and grime. He woofed again. 'Not without you' was clearly his message.

Bill hugged Corporal to him and buried his face in the wiry fur of the dog's neck, and let out a muffled sob. Only a few months ago, he attended Sunnington Down village school. Now here he was on the Western Front, risking death without ever having a real shot at a life.

"You did well, lad." Dyson removed one glove and laid a gentle hand on Bill's head. He felt a deep gash, the mousy brown hair sticky and covered in blood. He was just a boy, the rank of Sergeant or not. He had shown more bravery than most grown men would have in the same situation and the Lance Corporal felt real pity. A genuine feeling he had not felt since he had arrived in France.

There was no room for pity on the Western Front. Not if you wanted to remain sane and have any hope of getting home alive. He looked away.

"Let's get you back," he mumbled.

5.
DUTY

IT WAS LATE AUGUST 1915, and the sky was a clear deep blue, and the sun shone brightly. The Western Front was unusually quiet. There was no shelling by either side, no crack of rifle fire, not even the rat-tat-tat of machine guns. Both British and German soldiers were enjoying the last of Europe's summer warmth. Many took the opportunity to wash tunics and set up washing lines, write to loved ones and generally relax by sharing a bottle of wine with comrades while the going was good.

High above the trenches, two of those new-fangled flying machines were making lazy loops, chasing each other round and round in what seemed like an unending dance of one-upmanship. The drone of their engines rose and fell, but they were too high in the sky to bother the troops down on the ground.

Sergeant Bill Higgins and Corporal had caused quite a stir among the General Staff when news started to circulate of their heroic efforts in the tunnels some weeks before. Their actions resulted in the first Army Mine-Rescue School being formed in the small village of Strazeele just south of the French/Belgian border.

But as far as official recognition of the young Sergeant and his Airedale, there was nothing. Not even a well done. Not an officer, you see, sniffed the 'office wallah' toffs tucked safely 30 miles behind the front lines.

Not that Bill was even aware of any of this or would care even if he did. The gash in his head during the tunnel rescue had required 20 stitches, and Nurse Abigail Edgefield had him confined to a medical bunk at the field hospital for a week. Despite her better judgement when it came to hygiene, she allowed Corporal to come and go as he pleased. The Airedale Terrier spent hours lying quietly alongside Bill's bunk, and Nurse Abigail didn't have the heart to chase him out. If she was honest, that dog sometimes looked at her with eyes just daring her to try. She decided on discretion as the better part of valour and even fed Corporal when it was time for Bill's dinner.

"I can't thank you enough for being so kind to Corporal." Bill thanked Nurse Abigail once he was up and about and discharged as fit for full duties. "He really is very special, and I can't imagine being without him at my side for even an instant."

Bill then turned to his faithful friend. "Thank Nurse Abigail, Corporal, it is time to go."

Dutifully, Corporal let out two woofs and wagged his tail furiously before trotting out of the field hospital. As she watched them leave, the big-hearted nurse from Surrey kept her concerns well hidden.

The boy was beset by nightmares while he slept. Every night he babbled, thrashed in his sheets and was drenched in sweat. He had his demons all right, but then so did every injured man who was carried into the field hospital. The majority of them were young, too young to be tossed into the cauldron of war. Some had been so traumatised they just stared unmoving, totally catatonic. Others escaped their hospital bed restraints and ran off screaming in their nightshirts.

A few of these unfortunates were later found wandering by the Military Police and were court-martialled for cowardice for being far from their units and executed by firing squad. The barbarity of it was just another aspect of war over which the nurses and doctors had no influence.

Jim, Staff Sergeant McTaggart, had told her it would only get worse once the latest offensive was launched. The Allies' attack would be soon as supplies of ammunition and water were being built up in the forward areas just behind the trench network. A few miles further back in the heavy artillery emplacements, mountains of shells were also being stacked high, thousands of them.

A sure sign, an experienced McTaggart had told her, tapping the side of his nose in a gesture of confidential information.

"Take care, Bill and Corporal." Nurse Abigail waved to their retreating figures, but they did not turn around. They probably had not heard her farewell. Before returning to the other patients, a saddened Nurse Abigail briefly wondered if she would ever see the pair again. She knew it sounded cruel, but if anything happened to them, she hoped it would take them both out. It would break either of their hearts to be parted from the other.

At the top of the track, Mikey Doyle sat inside his motorised field ambulance. He waved to Nurse Abigail and handed a bottle of half-drunk red wine to Bill as he unslung his bolt-action Lee Enfield rifle. "It's not the best vintage, Bill, but all I could lay my hands on at short notice."

Bill and Corporal climbed into the vehicle, the young Sergeant taking a long pull from the bottle as he made himself as comfortable as the confines of the hard wooden cab would allow.

The dirt roads were abuzz with activity. A few motorised trucks belching smoke, engines backfiring, sending the horse-drawn wagons filled with ammunition boxes into a frenzy, soldiers cursing and shouting. It was a scene of organised chaos.

Doyle raced the engine and shot into the stream of traffic, which opened up miraculously before them. The large red crosses painted on the side of the motorised field ambulance had its advantages, and one of those was that everyone made way for the motor vehicle. Mikey Doyle was happy to take full advantage.

Corporal sat on the cab's bench seat between the two men. The weather had been free of rain for some weeks now, and the land had dried. Dirt roads now kicked up dust, and soldiers didn't have to wade through deep mud sucking at their boots like thick sticky toffee. There was a feeling of high spirits pervading the air. The field kitchens had moved closer to the front, and warmish meals were even getting delivered to the troops in the trenches. Life was good today for the ordinary British Tommy.

"Where did you get the wine, Yank?" Bill was just making small talk. He knew Yank was adept at acquiring almost anything. He had connections stretching as far back as Paris and even across the English Channel in London. Bill was aware he supplied the local Royal Flying Corps officers mess with genuine Scottish single malt whisky and, of course, gin and beer for the NCOs.

"Never you worry about that, Sergeant," Mikey gave him an irreverent salute, then looked across at his companion and winked. "I have a few more bottles in the back for you to share when you get back to your Berkshire Pals. Just don't get caught with the stuff, or you are on your own, Limey."

Although Limey was used as a disrespectful term to describe the English, Bill laughed it off and felt all the better for the addition of humour.

What was not funny were the solid ruts and potholes in the road. They threw the motorised field ambulance this way, then that way, and all in all, it was a very uncomfortable bone-jarring ride. Bill was quite relieved when they pulled off the track and came to a stop.

"I've got to pick up supplies, so I will be back here in about three hours, Bill. Just remember you do not have orders to be here, so head for your battalion's section of the trenches and don't hang about doing it, or the provosts will probably have you shot. And stay out of trouble."

Bill could hear Mikey's laughter as he pulled away back into the stream of traffic.

"Come on, Corporal." The young Sergeant with wine tucked away in his haversack and rifle slung over his shoulder headed for the nearest communication trench. John would love this stuff. He smiled, remembering when he and John had stolen one of his dad's bottles of wine and got drunk in the barn behind the church. He trusted John had more of a head for alcohol than he did then. He certainly had.

He didn't get excited often but was quite excited at the prospect of seeing his friends again. It had been six months at least since Sergeant Keane had given him new orders to report to American Field Hospital to bodyguard Corporal. And much had happened since then. But one thing he had made clear to the Corps of Engineers was neither he nor Corporal would be going back into those tunnels even if King George V himself was trapped down there.

The weeks of recovery had left Bill a very cynical young man, and he had every right. This war on the Western Front was little more than a meat grinder snatching the lives of the best of them.

Bill was not the same youth who, with best friend John Padfield, had marched off to war in search of adventure and glory. It had been a huge mistake, and Bill longed to see his village of Sunnington Down again, to be with his father and mother. To laze on his back by the village duck pond, watching streaks of cirrus cloud race through the sky. To then wander through John's door, see his best mate, and see his best friend's sister, Sissy, smile at him from the kitchen. She'd be sixteen now, old enough to walk out. He wondered how her hair fell now, whether it still fell in the same soft way on her shoulders. He wondered if he should write to her. She'd love to hear about Corporal. After the war, well after the war, perhaps Corporal and Pip would be the best of friends.

At the same time, Bill had grown up and was a man. He had responsibilities. He had his duty. He was highly trained to fight, kill and survive thanks to Staff Sergeant McTaggart. It was a case of doing or die. He was a Sergeant in His Majesty's British Expeditionary

Force in France battling to stop the Kaiser and his Hun army.

"Well, well. If I'm not mistaken, it's Sergeant Bill Higgins and his faithful companion, Corporal." Sergeant Albert Keane buried his surprise when a grim-faced Bill looked at him. The young sergeant's eyes lacked the sparkle of youth and were replaced by a chilling stare of indifference.

Keane looked the same: as red-faced as ever. Perhaps a little leaner.

"We are honoured this day. Come, Bill, I want a quick chat before you catch up with the rest of the lads. It's important."

Keane pulled back a canvas flap nailed to a wooden header that marked the entrance to the NCOs' bunker.

The wood log steps leading down had been hammered into the soil, so they were sturdy even if well-worn. The bunker was about 20 feet from the surface and reinforced with sandbags and thick staves driven into the soil to form a sort of roof. In the middle was a single wood table upon which a small candle provided light. There was a half-eaten loaf of bread and a small ham. Along the outside walls were bunks, two to a wall atop each other.

Bill sat down on a bench near the table and unslung his equipment.

"Fancy a sandwich?" Keane sat down with him and started slicing the bread. "No butter, though. Haven't seen any since we last had a rest rotation, and that was three weeks back."

He cut a slice of ham and passed it to Bill. In turn, the young Sergeant held it out to Corporal. They were both guests of Sergeant Keane, and Bill appreciated the fact that Corporal's standing was clearly acknowledged.

Bill dipped into his haversack and produced a bottle of wine. It was without a label, but that was a small detail and didn't matter to either a jot.

"I should have you two over for lunch more often," Keane laughed. He pulled out the cork with his teeth and splashed wine into two metal mugs. "Cheers. Your health Sergeant Higgins, and you, Corporal."

"Cheers, Sergeant Keane." They touched mugs and downed the wine.

"That's Sergeant-Major now, Higgins." Keane refilled the two mugs and flashed Bill a smile. "I dare say I will make Captain before this shindig is over. You will probably be a lieutenant before the year is out, Bill."

"Is it that bad, Sergeant-Major?"

"It is worse than bad, Bill." Keane filled the mugs again until the last drop of wine dribbled out. Bill pulled a second bottle from the haversack as Keane held the empty bottle by its neck like a club. "I think perhaps I can fill this with petrol, stuff the top with a rag, and it would make a fearsome surprise for the Huns. Burn the sods up good."

Bill was not feeling particularly hungry, but the wine warmed his belly.

Keane seemed somewhat preoccupied. Something was most definitely on his mind. The once larger-than-life man was now much diminished.

His voice was monotone. "John Padfield was killed yesterday." Keane did not look at Bill as if fearful of his reaction to the news of the death of his best friend since childhood. "I am sorry, Sergeant. At least it was quick. A sniper shot him through the head. He never knew what hit him."

"Shit happens, Sergeant-Major." It was all Bill could think to say in reply, and even to his ears, it sounded cold and callous. Besides, there was nothing he could do about it. John was gone. Just like many thousands of others.

"He was the fifth in the past seven days." Keane understood. He had been there himself and these days in the trenches made sure to make no friends. Here today gone tomorrow, the Sergeant-Major thought grimly. But he confessed he had an affection for the boy and his dog.

They were interrupted when a voice called into the bunker for Keane. There seemed some excitement and shouting above ground. Corporal joined in and started barking and racing around the bunker eagerly. The roar of mighty engines and rat-tat-tat of machine-gun fire filled the air and vibrated in their heads as they reached the open trenches. They were just in time to see two flying machines swoop upward, one chasing the other firing machine guns mercilessly. They must have come down to ground level during the dogfight, and it was clear the British Bristol Scout was having the worst of the kill-or-be-killed encounter. The biplane's red and blue roundels on the sides of the fabric covering wooden fuselage made a great target, and bullet holes could be seen clearly by the soldiers.

"Reconnaissance fighter escort, I'd guess." Keane and Bill watched the Bristol Scout start a rapid climb. The pilot could be seen clearly with his white scarf streaming out behind.

The German monoplane, with its sleek single wing and menacing iron cross painted on its side and wings, was faster and much more deadly.

The single-seat Fokker Eindecker was the pride of the Imperial German Air Service. It had been rushed into service early in June and set about decimating the Royal Flying Corps with its interrupter gear technology, allowing it to fire through the propellers without any damage.

A groan went up from the British trenches as the Bristol Scout's engine spluttered at the top of its climb. There was a chattering of machine-gun fire from the chasing Fockker, and white smoke burst from the British machine.

"Poor chap. They do not even have parachutes." Keane turned away from the certain death of the Royal Flying Corps pilot. It would not be pretty, and he had seen enough of death not to want to watch one more.

Bill was quite fascinated. He had never seen a dogfight before. He had heard of them and seen the flying machines landing and taking off from the aerodrome a few miles from the American Field Hospital.

Many soldiers in the trenches regularly applied to join the Royal Flying Corps. They saw it as a way out.

As he watched, the Bristol Scout rolled over and hurtled earthward, trailing thick smoke. Just when everyone thought it was going to hit the German trenches, the nose came up, and the biplane skidded sideways through the air engine roaring and propellers whirring. It was a do or die attempt to reach the British lines.

Bill joined the other soldiers in yelling the pilot on to success while the Huns opened fire on the biplane with rifles and machine guns as it skimmed no man's land.

One of the wheels of the Bristol Scout's fixed landing gear caught the remains of a barbed wire fence and sent the aircraft crashing into the ground. It skidded to the left, lost its right-wing and then rolled over.

For a moment, all was quiet then with a crunching noise, what was left of the crumpled biplane slid into a shell hole in the middle of no man's land. Smoke drifted out of the crater, and one of the Bristol Scout's wings pointed skyward like a lone grave marker.

There was no movement. The victorious Fokker was nowhere to be seen. Life in the trenches went back to the daily routine. The dogfight and death of the pilot no more than a temporary distraction. Gruesome entertainment.

Bill stopped himself from turning away. Who said the pilot was dead? He could be badly injured and in need of rescue and medical attention. As loath to as he was, the young Sergeant knew there was nothing for it but to send Corporal to find out. Their duty was clear.

"Corporal," he sighed.

Bill felt a nudge and looked down to see the Airedale Terrier standing next to him with the Mercy Dog medic kit harness in his mouth. He had taken it from the open haversack in the dugout. The dog knew before he did.

Bill buckled on the harness and called for his rifle. "Okay, Corporal, let's go."

Bill helped Corporal to one of the observation slots which overlooked the German trenches, and the terrier was gone in a flash. The young Sergeant pushed his rifle through the same slot keeping half an eye on where the plane had crashed and an eye on the German lines.

There was no gunfire, but Bill could see no sign of Corporal either. A heavy hand pulled him down from the firing step of the slot.

"You want to get killed, Sergeant?" The anger in Keane's voice was there for all in the trench to hear. "That is exactly where and how we lost John Padfield; your friend John Padfield. Snipers target these slots just waiting for fools like you to peer out."

Bill shrugged off Keane's grip and leaned forward, so he was mere inches from the Sergeant Major's face. He said nothing but the message of imminent violence was clear if anyone prevented Bill from protecting Corporal.

Keane stepped backwards in surprise. This was no longer the pimply youth he had led out of the trenches all those months ago. He had heard about the rescue in the tunnels, and Keane knew that took real courage. Sergeant Bill Higgins was now a very capable and dangerous soldier.

At that moment, Corporal came diving through the slot at breakneck speed and knocked Bill clean off the firing step to the bottom of the trench. He had been in no man's land for only a few minutes.

Corporal was good at this search and rescue stuff. In his mouth, he had a whitish scarf reminiscent of the one which had streamed behind the Bristol Scout's pilot as he had futilely tried to climb to escape the German Fokker.

"What does that mean?" Keane asked.

His near confrontation was forgotten. Bill picked himself up and dusted down his uniform.

"It means the pilot is alive, Sargeant-Major," Bill's answer was unexpected, but Mercy Dogs were trained to bring back a piece of clothing, a hat, scarf to show they had found a survivor. Time was critical now.

The crucial thing Corporal could not reveal was how badly injured the man was. One of his medic canvas bags was open, and the flask on his back was gone. The downed pilot was alive and right under the German guns in no man's land.

6.
GLORY

"HOLD IT RIGHT THERE, SERGEANT HIGGINS." Both Keane and Bill turned at the sound of the command. Just below where they stood on the firing step was Lieutenant Anthony Smythe.

Smythe looked as if he had just come from a parade. His uniform was immaculate, brass shoulder pips gleamed, and the faint shadow on his top lip revealed the nineteen-year-old's aspirations of a moustache.

"Correct me if I am wrong, Sergeant Major Keane, but Higgins here is still a part of C Company, and I am still his commanding officer. Right?"

Keane shot a glance at Bill, half expecting an insubordinate response from the young Sergeant. None came, and Keane breathed a sigh of relief.

"That is correct, Lieutenant." Keane stepped down into the trench and threw Lieutenant Smythe a crisp salute. "The Sergeant is still part of the Berkshire Pals, sir. Currently, Sergeant Higgins has command orders to bodyguard the Mercy Dog Corporal and to perform any special duties in relation to those orders, Sir."

"I am well aware of Higgins' orders, and I am also well aware the term 'special duties' give him virtually carte blanche to do what the bloody hell he wants." Smythe's dry laugh caught both William and Keane off guard, and neither man was quite sure how to react. "On the other hand, *you chaps*, it does not give him the right to deprive His Majesty of a brave soldier by getting himself killed, *what?*"

Smythe motioned to the two men, and they followed him down the wood stave steps into the gloom of the nearby NCOs' bunker. The half-full bottle of red wine, the ham and some slices of bread were still sitting on the table alongside the two mugs.

It was one thing to tangle with Sergeant Major Keane but disobeying a commissioned officer giving a direct order was a firing squad offence, and Bill knew it too.

He clamped his mouth firmly shut. Whatever happened here, the young Sergeant would do his duty and try and rescue the downed airman. Corporal had risked his life to find out if the pilot had survived the dogfight and crash and brought the dirty white scarf back as proof. He wouldn't let Corporal down. Whatever this toff said.

Smythe sat on the bench and crossed his legs showing highly polished brown custom-made leather boots. He reached down to his leather holster, withdrew his service revolver, and placed it on the wood table. The top-break Webley .455 was one of the most powerful revolvers ever produced and a standard piece of kit for all British Officers. Purchased at their own expense, of course. After all, they were officers and were expected to maintain certain standards, especially when it came to paying their mess bills.

"Sit down, Gentlemen." Smythe waved his hand to the bench opposite. "There are two types of heroes in this war. One is the stupid hero who ends up shot to bits and very dead. Then there is the second type. The hero who still puts his life on the line but does so with a certain amount of calculation and a hell of a lot of luck. You feel lucky today by any chance, Sergeant Higgins?"

He squinted, inadvertently copying his deceased Captain's expression. Whether Sidney Wellsworth-Pike had died for stupidity or lack of luck was not known. But he had died. Nevermore to read or recite Homer:

This was the first time since the battalion had been formed that any officer had ever spoken to him directly, and William was a little taken aback.

Lieutenant Smythe was no fool. Everyone in the Company knew his background of leaving Oxford University to join up to fight. It was rumoured he had been studying philosophy and classical Greek. He was very much the toff but had a good reputation for fairly treating the men under his command.

Bill looked at Keane, who ignored the sidelong glance.

"No need to answer me, Higgins." Lieutenant Smythe pulled a small flask from inside his tunic. He removed the top and turned it upside down, and poured himself a dram.

Bill could smell the sweet liquor from across the table.

"American Bourbon, Higgins. Got a few cases from the American Embassy in Paris. Know a chap with connections, you see."

Another one of Mikey Doyle's acquaintances, no doubt, thought Bill.

Smythe did not sip the bourbon. Instead, he threw it back in one straight movement and swallowed.

It was quite obvious this was a regular occurrence with the young Lieutenant. Bill did not blame him. In fact, he was sympathetic, having resorted to Dutch courage on more than one occasion himself. And since his return from the tunnels, a few cases of wine a week helped him sleep. Smuggled past Nurse Abigail and courtesy of Mikey Doyle, of course.

"Enough of that. Now, where was I?"

"Calculation and a hell of a lot of luck, Sir." Keane prompted him in an effort to find out what the officer wanted. You did not find them often in the trenches with the enlisted men. That is what the NCOs were there for, and their mere presence made everyone uneasy.

"Right. Now listen carefully, Higgins." Smythe sat up straight and tapped his middle finger on the table. "I know you are going to try and see what you can do for that chap in the flying machine. And a jolly good show to you for having the courage to do so, I say. You can step out there right now and have your damned fool head shot off, or you can listen to what I have to say and at least stand some sort of chance of seeing the sun rise tomorrow.'

He paused dramatically. "What do you say? Let me explain."

Lieutenant Anthony Smythe might be an alcoholic, but he certainly had brains for toff and a lot of cunning, and it was all wrapped up in a tidy package of logic.

Sergeant Major Keane went off to find a long pole and white flag once the plan was agreed upon. Smythe pushed his Webley service revolver along the table to Bill, who immediately took it and shoved it in his uniform trouser belt at his back and flipped his tunic over to hide it from sight.

As Smythe pointed out, if he went into no man's land with his rifle, the Huns would more likely than not shoot him. There again, he could not go unarmed hence the revolver.

"You ready?" Smythe indicated the half-drunk bottle of wine on the table. "Do not forget to take that and do not forget to be seen taking swigs of it when you are in no man's land. It could be the difference between life and death, Higgins. Good luck, Sergeant."

Smythe disappeared, and William grabbed up the wine and headed back to the trench where Corporal was waiting for him.

The terrier was going to be a bit of a problem. There was no way Bill could see Corporal not wanting to follow him in. After all, he was trained as a Mercy Dog, among other things. He was his shadow.

Sergeant Major Keane was waiting for him with a long pole and white flag, looking a bit sceptical. Corporal sat next to him, eyeing the situation. He knew there was something going on. He woofed at Bill, who shook his head.

"Not this time, Corporal. You stay here with Albert, there's a good boy, and I'll be back in a jiffy."

Corporal growled, and Bill bent down and stroked his neck and shoulders. Corporal woofed and licked his face to return the affection. Bill felt his heart breaking. "Please, Corporal. Just wait for me. You have done your bit now; it is my turn. So stay here, you hear? You gotta stay safe."

Keane sat down with Corporal and hung his arm around the terrier's shoulders in case he needed to tighten his grip. But it was not necessary. The Corporal understood perfectly.

The Corporal cocked his head and watched as Bill clambered over the top of the trench sandbags and disappeared from view.

It was a good plan, brilliant even. This sector of the front had been quiet all day. Soldiers on both sides enjoyed the warmth and bright blue sky, and no one wanted to start a fight. The guns were silent, and men were at peace, at least for today. Tomorrow there would be time enough for war. The flying machine dogfight going on overhead had been ignored by everyone until it literally landed in their faces. Even then, the action was so sudden it was over before it had even begun for the troops relaxing in and behind the trenches.

The broken Bristol Scout was in pieces in a shell crater. The wreck had stopped giving off smoke, and its lone wing thrust upright was now just part of the war-torn landscape along with the barbed wire and everything else in No Man's Land. No one was taking any notice as the pilot had never emerged into the open, and no one had spotted Corporal's dash there and back either.

Bill scrambled unsteadily to his feet and staggered forward into no man's land waving the white flag. He stopped for a moment and took a long swig of red wine. At that moment, it was the best wine ever to pass his lips.

Bill felt as if every German gun was being pointed at him. His skin crawled, and the hairs on the back of his neck stood up. Every pore in his body opened, and he was drenched in sweat in seconds. Fear. This was a real fear of imminent death. What he had felt in the tunnels paled in comparison to this.

He took a step forward and then another.

"Hey there." He shouted in a slurred voice. He could see a few heads popping up in the German trenches, and he took another swig of wine. But he was stone-cold sobre. "Whitey flaggy. You Huns, understandy."

Bill staggered forward a few more paces, slowly angling towards the shell hole containing the downed flying machine and the wounded pilot.

"You crazy drunk on schnapps Tommy!" The shout in broken English came from the German trenches, followed by raucous, deep laughter. There was a single rifle shot, but the bullet came nowhere near him. That didn't stop Bill from almost vomiting, but he kept his nerve and kept staggering along waving his flag.

The bullet was just some German having fun to scare the 'drunkard Tommy', he suspected, he hoped.

Bill tripped and went sprawling, followed by gales of laughter from both the British and German trenches. He managed to land on his back with his arm in the air, safely clutching the wine bottle which drew whistles and calls of encouragement. Whatever happens, do not drop the booze seemed to be the sentiment on both sides.

Climbing to his feet, Bill took another swig and dusted down his uniform. He picked up the pole with its white flag and, waving it aloft, staggered the final 20 feet to the lip of the smouldering shell crater.

Lieutenant Smythe's plan was working a treat. Bill's drunken act and white flag were more a fun spectacle than a threat. There was no doubt among the soldiers looking on that this lone Tommy was drunk as a lord and had got it into his head to grab a souvenir from the downed flying machine.

It was one of those rare moments of humanity and humour in war that no one could account for. It was one thing to shoot down a soldier, the enemy, but quite another to kill a drunk on a glorious summer's day. Bill made sure he fell head-first into the crater before rolling over and sitting up.

"Glad to see you didn't spill the wine, old boy." The pilot stretched out before him and looked in a bad way. There was blood trickling from his mouth, which probably indicated a punctured lung. Bill could see his right foot was missing, and a crude tourniquet had been self-applied to stem the bleeding.

"Give me that bottle, will you?"

Bill handed it over and watched the wounded aviator gulp it down. He gave the young Sergeant a lopsided grin. "You don't happen to have anything stronger on you, do you? My right foot hurts like buggery."

Bill handed over his silver flask given to him by Staff Sergeant James McTaggart. It was filled with the finest French brandy that Mikey Doyle could get his hands on.

Pulling out the medic canvas bag usually reserved for Corporal's mercy harness, Bill cleaned the bloody stump and dressed the open wound.

"That your dog earlier? A blessing it was, I can tell you." The pilot still had his leather flying helmet on and his goggles firmly over his eyes. His Bristol Scout was nothing more than a collection of fabric, wood, and wires and the engine and what was left of the propeller lay to one side. The wing sticking up into the sky was wedged firmly against the remains of the fuselage tail and the side of the shell crater.

"You are going to be okay. It looks like there's little bleeding." Bill nodded his head, indicating the British trenches. "All we have to do is wait for dark, and then I'll carry you back to our lines and the medics there."

The pilot eyed him and took another long, greedy swig.

"There's a beautiful nurse there; she will look after you better than any angel ever would." Bill hesitated and remembered his stay in hospital.

The pilot eyed him. "She got–?" He mimed large breasts and a tiny waist.

It felt wrong to talk about Sister Edgefield in that manner, but Bill grinned to humour the pilot and maintain his spirits. "She's beautiful, mate."

"Nice," whistled the pilot wistfully.

"Just stay awake till nightfall."

The calm in Bill's voice surprised him. He had felt fearful on his stumbling trek across no man's land pretending to be a crazy drunk. The Lieutenant had been right in his assessment of the situation, and his plan had worked a treat. Now all they had to do was follow the second part of that plan and wait until dark, and they would be home free.

"No. Sorry, old boy, that just won't do." The pilot shook his head and pushed a square metal box towards Bill. "You go now, or you don't go at all, and that would be a disaster."

"I do not follow what you mean, sir."

This pilot was a toff but no soft office wallah. The pain of his decimated foot must be incredible, almost unbearable by any standard, but the man spoke with a steady calm tone.

"You do not have to understand, Sergeant. You just have to carry out my orders. You pick up that metal box and get back to the British lines like the devil himself was after you. No arguments. Now get going, and that is an order!"

The pilot fell back against the side of the crater. He had momentarily passed out, and Bill moved to his side to wake him. Order or no order, there was no way he was going to leave an injured man behind.

The pilot regained consciousness and grabbed the Sergeant's arm.

"Listen to me. In two days, the General High Command will launch an attack in this sector. My mission was to fly reconnaissance and take photographs of the enemy's positions. Those photographs are vital to the attack's success, and they are in this metal box."

Again, the pilot pushed the box towards Bill.

It was beginning to dawn on the young Sergeant that thousands of soldiers' lives were at stake, and the pilot was right.

"But if I leave now, I won't get ten yards. The Huns will fill me full of holes." Bill shook his head to underline his point. "The plan is to wait until dark, then start back."

"Sorry, Sergeant, but if you stay here much longer, you are a dead man anyway. There is no glory in war, only death and destruction."

Just then, a shell exploded off to the right of the crater near the German trenches. The peaceful day was now good and truly shattered.

"A ranging shot," explained the pilot. "That Fokker pilot who shot me down knew what I was doing. He knew I was photographing artillery parks, ammunition dumps and railways."

The pilot leaned forward and coughed up a stream of blood. Bill had to get him back behind the lines right now. There was no way he would last until nightfall.

Two more shells exploded in quick succession. Each came nearer and nearer to the crater in which the pilot and Bill were sheltered.

"He would have called in the artillery to blow this plane, and its contents to kingdom come. You understand?"

Another shell exploded with the force of a hurricane and slammed Bill to the ground. There was a ringing in his ears, and pain stabbed his left side.

Shrapnel, no doubt. His hand came away covered in blood. There was no more time. The next shell would hit them square on.

The young Sergeant pulled the pilot forward and hiked him over his shoulders. He then picked up the metal box and started up the side of the crater.

He felt strangely calm. He knew what he had to do, and he was going to do it.

He had promised Corporal he would be back, and William Higgins kept his promises.

No sooner had he emerged from the crater in no man's land than bullets started to zip and buzz all around. Bill raised his head and could see return fire coming from the British lines. They were doing everything possible to keep the German's heads down while Bill made his dash for safety.

If only they knew the vital information he carried. Intelligence which would save the lives of his Berkshire Pal's Battalion. Many, many lives.

Bill staggered on. He felt bullets strike the pilot on his back again and again. The man was obviously now dead, but his body, despite the weight, could still shield himself from the rifle fire.

Watching through the sandbag observation slit, Sergeant Major Keane followed Bill's painfully slow progress. The Corporal stared intently at his master, longing to go to him but knowing he had been commanded to stay. Torn, the dog whinnied and pawed.

The young Sergeant was bent almost double with the weight of the injured pilot. The men were on the firing step and shooting round after round at the Germans at Keane's direction.

Machine-gun fire broke out on both sides. No one knew what was happening except that fighting had broken out once more.

The artillery shells started to come in thick and fast. The Germans obviously thought it was a British attack, a possible probe of their front lines.

Keane watched one shell land directly in the crater where he had seen Bill with the pilot slung across his back had been moments before. The wreck of the Bristol Scout disappeared completely as if it had never been there. Another shell exploded to the front of the crater, and then a third landed with a *crruummp* to the front of Sergeant Keane, obscuring Bill and the pilot.

When the smog of the explosive shell cleared, there was no sign of them. Where Bill and the pilot should have been was just a smoking crater.

The shelling stopped abruptly, and the firing died down on both sides. Sergeant William 'Bill' Higgins was dead. Vapourised by the heavy artillery round.

Keane fell back in shock.

No, no, no. Bill couldn't be gone.

But he was.

Corporal lifted his head to the sky and let out a long mournful howl full of sorrow and heartbreak.

The intensity of the big terrier's howls echoed across no man's land and among the trenches, and no one within hearing was immune to the sheer pain and anguish they carried.

Sergeant Major Keane pulled a shaking Corporal closer as Bill's best friend continued to howl and howl and howl louder and louder his lament of grief and loss.

EPILOGUE

Dear Mama

I am safe and well, and I sincerely hope that the money I send home is helping you, my brother Robert and little Lucy.

Thank you for the photographic images of you all. I wish I was there with you right now.

There has been a major battle, and I am working night and day helping the wounded. There are so many injured I have them piled up everywhere on my motorised field ambulance. There are even more walking wounded struggling to get to the forward field hospitals.

I do not know how much more of this carnage, this slaughter, I can endure. After this latest British attack, the bodies were so thick on the ground that I could have walked right up to the German trenches without stepping on a single patch of earth.

Do you remember the Airedale Terrier I wrote you about? The Mercy Dog Corporal? He truly is a wonder. He must have saved over 30 injured soldiers that the stretcher-bearers had left for dead on the battlefield. He is truly a remarkable animal.

I am sorry to tell you that the young Sergeant Higgins I wrote you about is also among the dead. He was killed just two days before the battle, trying to rescue a crashed Royal Flying Corps pilot. I wasn't there to see him die, and I thank the Good Lord for such a small mercy. He was my friend and Corporal's friend too. But neither of us have had time to mourn his loss, and the only way I can get through the day is with Corporal by my side and to pretend William - Bill - is still alive somewhere.

When he's not working, the Corporal lies on the mound of earth that is William's grave as if to keep the 18-year-old's body warm.

I feel so guilty to be living when so many are dead. I curse the old men on all sides who send young men and mere boys to fight and die in their wars. I pray every night that our great country of the United States of America never gets drawn into this crime against God's children. War is the devil's work; of that, I now have no doubt.

I will write to you again soon. I have to go now. I must collect Corporal's new bodyguard. He'll be the fifth in just 18 months.

May God have mercy on his soul as he is surely marked for death.

Your loving son,

Mikey Doyle

12 October 2015

Field Ambulance Medic

American Ambulance Hospital

North-West of Paris

Printed in Great Britain
by Amazon